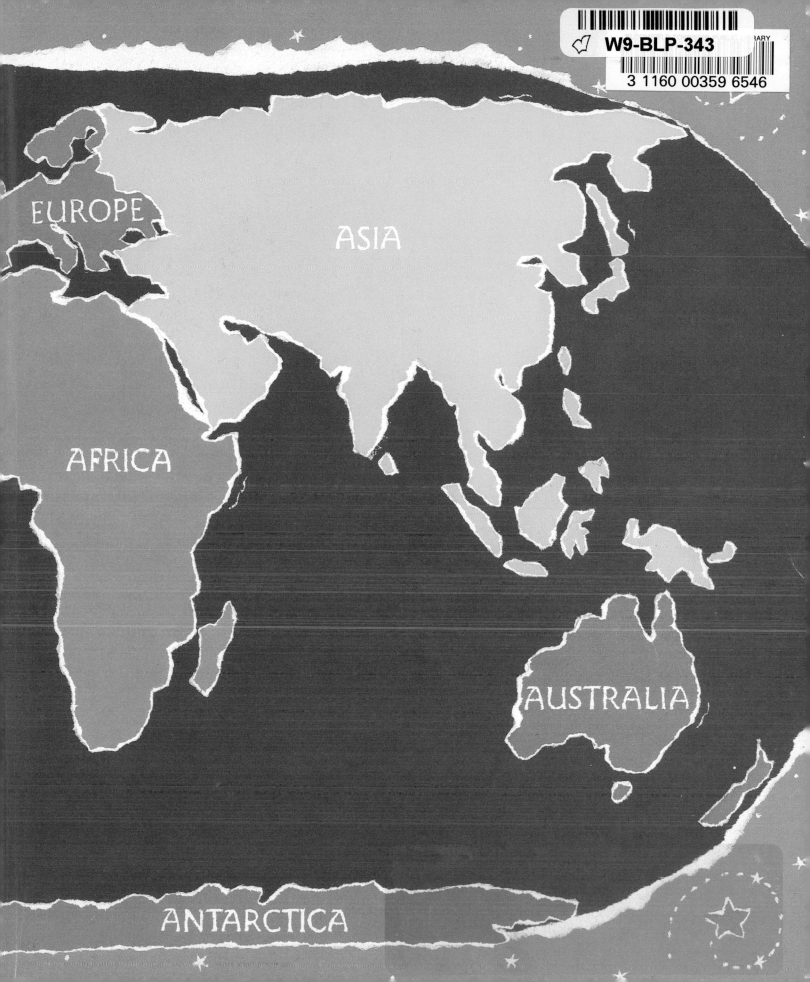

EUROPE

ASIA

AFRICA

AUSTRALIA

ANTARCTICA

Sleep, Sleep, Sleep

A Lullaby for Little Ones Around the World

by **Nancy Van Laan**

Pictures by Holly Meade

Little, Brown and Company
Boston   New York   Toronto   London

For my son, David, who started this ritual
N. V. L.

For my affectionate niece, Hilary
H. M.

All of the foreign words in this book are spelled phonetically, and each expresses a particular culture's way of saying, "Good night, go to sleep, little one." The cultures and languages represented are, in order of appearance: Navajo; Botswana/Setswana; Norway/Norwegian; Bolivia/Spanish; China/Cantonese; Chile/Spanish (because of the Chilean research base in Antarctica); and Australia/English.

Text copyright © 1995 by Nancy Van Laan
Illustrations copyright © 1995 by Holly Meade

First Edition

Library of Congress Cataloging-in-Publication Data

Van Laan, Nancy.
  Sleep, sleep, sleep : a lullaby for little ones around the world / by Nancy Van Laan ; pictures by Holly Meade.
— 1st ed.
    p.   cm.
  Summary: Illustrations and rhythmic verses depict a mother and child and different animals on each of the seven continents.
  ISBN 0-316-89732-9
  [1. Lullabies. 2. Mother and child — Fiction. 3. Animals — Fiction.] I. Meade, Holly, ill. II. Title.
PZ7.V3269Sl 1995
[E] — dc20   93-44484

10 9 8 7 6 5 4 3 2 1

SC

Published simultaneously in Canada by Little, Brown & Company (Canada) Limited and in Great Britain by Little, Brown and Company (UK) Limited

Printed in Hong Kong

The pictures for this book were created with torn paper. The white outline around many of the shapes is achieved by gently tearing papers that are colored on one side and white on the other. Handmade papers, such as Elephant Hide and Wrinkled Peach, have also been used. Pieces are arranged and then glued. Detail is added by scraping through the colored surface with a sharp point.

Way out in the country,
Mother lullabies her baby.
She sings to her little one:
Ith-wush, ith-wush, ith-wush.
Sleep, sleep, sleep.

NORTH AMERICA

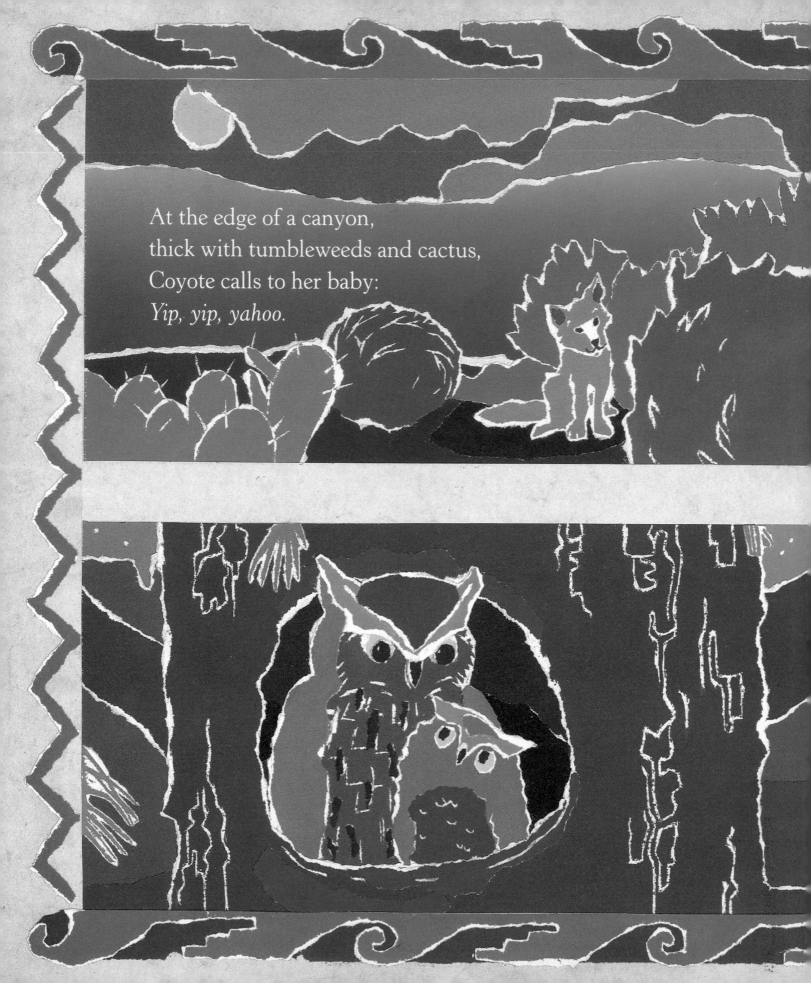

At the edge of a canyon,
thick with tumbleweeds and cactus,
Coyote calls to her baby:
Yip, yip, yahoo.

Peeking out a hole,
in a piñon near a mesa,
Owl hoots to her baby:
Whoo, whoo, whoo.

In another land afar,
Mother lullabies her baby.
She sings to her little one:
Robala, robala, robala.
Sleep, sleep, sleep.

High up on a steep cliff,
standing proud and tall,
Leopard soothes her baby:
Purr, purr, purr.

Stepping through the tall grass,
dining on the leaves,
Giraffe tends her baby:
Nibba, nibba, nibba.

In another land afar,
Mother lullabies her baby.
She sings to her little one:
Sove, sove, sove.
Sleep, sleep, sleep.

EUROPE

Deep inside a mountain,
in a dark, cozy cavern,
Brown Bear lulls her baby:
Grr, grr, grr.

At the end of a meadow,
beneath a mound of snow,
Rabbit feeds her baby:
Munch, munch, munch.

In another land afar,
Mother lullabies her baby.
She sings to her little one:
Dwair-may, dwair-may, dwair-may.
Sleep, sleep, sleep.

SOUTH AMERICA

Nestled in some palm fronds,
swaying side to side,
Parrot murmurs to her baby:
Tchh, tchh, tchh.

High up in a tree,
slipping in between the vines,
Boa slithers with her baby:
Hiss, hiss, hiss.

In another land afar,
Mother lullabies her baby.
She sings to her little one:
Fun gao, fun gao, fun gao leh.
Sleep, sleep, sleep.

At the edge of a river,
lighted by the moon,
Deer drinks with her baby:
S-sip, s-sip, s-sip.

Over in the mountains,
in a forest of bamboo,
Panda rests with her baby:
Sh, sh, sh.

In another land afar,
Mother lullabies her baby.
She sings to her little one:
Sway-nya, sway-nya, sway-nya.
Sleep, sleep, sleep.

Drifting on an ice floe,
in the quiet sea,
Seal glides with her baby:
Arf, arf, arf.

Bobbling in the ocean,
rolling to and fro,
Whale swims with her baby:
Sha-wish, sha-wish, sha-wish.

In another land afar,
Mother lullabies her baby.
She sings to her little one:
Sleep, sleep, sleep.

In the dark, damp forest,
full of moss-covered stumps,
Kangaroo hops with her baby:
Thump, thump, thump.

Climbing up a gum tree,
snapping off the bark,
Koala crawls with her baby:
Wah, wah, wah.

All around the world,
mothers lullaby their babies.
They sing to their little ones:

Yip, yip, yahoo.

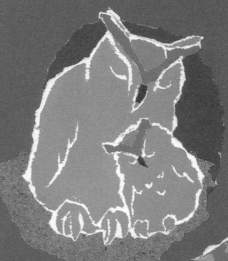

Whoo, whoo, whoo.

Nibba, nibba, nibba.

Purr, purr, purr.

Grr, grr, grr.

Munch, munch, munch.

Tchh, tchh, tchh.

Hiss, hiss, hiss.

S-sip, s-sip, s-sip.

Sh, sh, sh.

Arf, arf, arf.

Sha-wish, sha-wish, sha-wish.

Thump, thump, thump.

Wah, wah, wah.

Sleep, sleep, sleep.

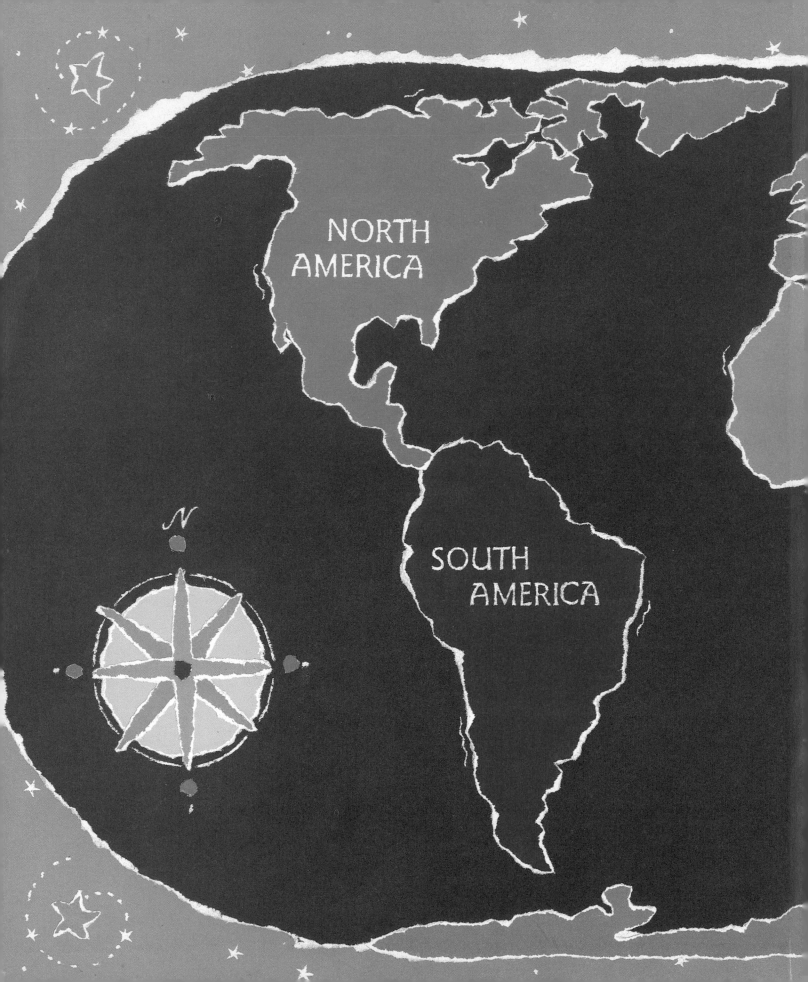